Cookies and Crutches

Cookies and Crutches

JUDY DELTON

Illustrated by Alan Tiegreen

A YEARLING BOOK

Published by
Bantam Doubleday Dell Books for Young Readers
a division of
Bantam Doubleday Dell Publishing Group, Inc.
1540 Broadway
New York, New York 10036

The trademarks Yearling® and Dell® are registered in the U.S. Patent and Trademark Office and in other countries.

ISBN: 0-440-40010-4

Printed in the United States of America

July 1988

30 29 28 27 26 25 24 23 22 21

OPM

For Dyana Peters,
who has Pee Wee Scouts of her own

Contents

Contents

CHAPTER 1

Three O'clock at Last

Molly Duff watched the clock.

The big black minute hand dropped, boing, boing, boing.

One minute at a time.

To get to three o'clock, it had to climb, chug, chug, chug.

At three o'clock the bell would ring.

The Pee Wee Scouts from first grade would run out of the room and down the stairs. They were in Troop 23.

Clop, clop, clop.

Tuesday was their meeting day.

Molly could not wait.

Today Mrs. Peters would show them how to bake cookies.

Mmm. Molly felt hungry thinking about it.

She could not sit still in her seat on Tuesdays.

She pretended to think very hard about her spelling words.

She squinted and said, "Pig: p-i-g."

But she was not thinking about *pig*.

She was thinking about Scouts and cookies.

Molly knew how to spell.

She could spell *pig* without thinking at all.

Spelling was easy.

"Mary Beth, spell *home*," said Mrs. Lane.

Mary Beth Kelly was passing a note to
Sonny Betz.

Mrs. Lane watched for people who
passed notes.

Mary Beth turned red.
She was not good at spelling.
"Spell *home*," Mrs. Lane said again.

3

"Home-comb," said Molly to herself.
"Let's go to Scouts!"

Mrs. Lane looked as if she wanted to leave too.

She spelled *home* for Mary Beth.

"Keep your eyes on your spelling, Mary Beth," said Mrs. Lane.

"Yes, Mrs. Lane," said Mary Beth.

Molly looked at the clock. Chug, chug, chug.

The big hand was climbing to three.

"Home," said Mrs. Lane. "It is almost time to go home!"

Sonny Betz waved his hand.

"Not for us!" he said.

"It is Tuesday. We have Scouts on Tuesday."

"Dear me, I forgot!" said Mrs. Lane.

Teachers were not supposed to forget, thought Molly.

That was a teacher's job. To remember everything.

It was good that the first graders remembered it was Tuesday.

Remembered it was Scout day.

Or else Mrs. Peters would be all alone with her cookies.

Gobble, gobble, gobble.

Mrs. Peters would eat all the cookies herself!

Dozens and dozens of cookies!

Molly laughed into her speller thinking about it.

The minute hand was still climbing. Chug, chug, chug.

"Row One, get your coats," said Mrs. Lane.

Row One raced to the back of the room.

"Row Two is noisy," said Mrs. Lane. "I will call on Row Three because they are quiet."

Row Three raced to the back of the room.

Molly sat up straight. She sat very very still. She was in Row Two.

Mrs. Lane looked at Molly.

"Row Two," she said.

Row Two got their coats.

Some of the children got in line.

Then Mrs. Lane called, "Pee Wee Scouts, line up!"

*   *   *

The minute hand climbed its last minute.
It was on the twelve.
The bell rang, BRRRING!

Molly covered her ears. The bell was right outside the first-grade door!
The lines marched out of the room.
It was time for Pee Wee Scouts at last!
It was time to learn how to bake cookies.

CHAPTER 2

Raw Dough!

Troop 23 ran all the way down the stairs.
The school bus waited near the door.
Molly wanted to get there first.
She squeezed ahead of Mary Beth Kelly.
Then she squeezed ahead of Sonny Betz.
But Rachel Myers was there first.
She was in the other first grade.

"That's not fair," said Molly. "Your room is closer to the door."
"I can run faster," said Rachel.

"I've got my running shoes on."

Molly looked at Rachel's running shoes. Everybody had some.

Everybody but Molly.

Molly's mother said running shoes were not school shoes.

"A hex on your running shoes," said Molly, crossing her eyes.

Molly said that when she was mad.

It made her feel better.

It scared some people.

They thought she might really put a hex on them.

But she couldn't.

A hex was not a real thing.

The Scouts got on the school bus.

They got off at Mrs. Peters's house.

Mrs. Peters was waiting at the door.

"We'll meet in the kitchen today," she said.

The Scouts followed her one by one.

She had bowls and spoons out.
She had flour and butter and sugar.
"Umm," said Molly, rubbing her stomach.

Everyone stood around the table.
They all wanted to be in front.
They all wanted to see.
Mostly, they all wanted a cookie!

Mrs. Peters smiled.
She was friendly and kind.
She was a good troop leader.

"Before we begin, does anyone have a good deed to report?" Mrs. Peters asked the Scouts.

"I helped my grandma wash her windows this week," said Sonny Betz.

"Good!" said Mrs. Peters.

"I carried three bags of groceries for the lady next door," said Roger White.

"Wonderful," said Mrs. Peters. "You've been real Pee Wees this week. Today, I will show you how to make easy cookies.

"To earn your cookie badge, you must bake cookies yourself.

"You must bake them at home and bring one to me.

"I will see if you earn the badge.

"Your parents must not help.

"But they must know you are using the stove.

"And they must write a note saying you baked them yourselves.

"Do you all understand what to do?"

The Scouts nodded.

All except Roger White.

"Baking cookies is for girls," he said.

"It is not," said Sonny Betz.

"Sissy!" said Roger. "Mama's boy!"

Lots of people thought Sonny was a sissy.

His mother still walked to school with him every morning.

She met him after school too.

Mrs. Peters held up her hand.

"Do you like to eat, Roger?" she said.

Roger nodded.

"If boys can eat, boys can cook," she said. "Baking and cooking are for everyone."

"Yeah!" shouted Sonny. "I told you, creep!"

Mrs. Peters began to measure flour.
She explained the measuring cups.
And the measuring spoons.
She mixed the butter and sugar.
She put in eggs.
She put in flour.
She mixed it all up.

At the end she put in chocolate chips and nuts.

"Umm," said Molly and Mary Beth together.

"I could eat them right now. Before they are baked," said Rachel.

Roger made gagging noises.

"You can't eat raw flour," he said. "Yuck!"

"And raw eggs," said Molly. "Right out of a chicken!"

"It's good!" said Rachel. "I could eat that whole bowl of dough right now!"

Now everyone was making gagging sounds.

Mrs. Peters had to hold her hand up again.

She showed the Scouts how to scoop the dough with a teaspoon and put it on

the pan. When the pan was full, she put it into the oven.

"Now!" she said. "We put the timer on for twelve minutes. While we wait, we will sing our Pee Wee Scout song!"

Troop 23 got into a circle.

Mrs. Peters washed her hands at the sink.

Everybody sang.

♪ ♪ ♪ **Pee Wee Song** ♪ ♪ ♪

(to the tune of
"Old MacDonald Had a Farm")

Scouts are helpers, Scouts have fun,
Pee Wee, Pee Wee Scouts!
We sing and play when work is done,
Pee Wee, Pee Wee Scouts!

With a good deed here,
And an errand there,
Here a hand, there a hand,
Everywhere a good hand.

Scouts are helpers, Scouts have fun,
Pee Wee, Pee Wee Scouts!

While the Scouts sang, they sniffed the air.

The cookies smelled wonderful, baking.

CHAPTER **3**

Root Beer to the Rescue

When the cookies were done, Mrs. Peters gave one to each Scout.

"Umm," said Molly. "These are good cookies!"

The cookies were warm and soft.

The chocolate chips were melted and ran down the Scouts' fingers.

"See if you can make good cookies too," said Mrs. Peters.

"Be sure your mother is home. Be careful when you use the stove."

Mrs. Peters passed out papers.
They were recipes for how to make the cookies.

~~~~~~

 Pee Wee Cookies

3/4 cup brown sugar
3/4 cup white sugar
1 cup butter
2 eggs
2 tsp. vanilla

Mix well.

Then add: 1 tsp. baking soda
1 tsp. salt

20

2 cups flour
1 cup oatmeal
2 cups cornflakes
1 pkg. chocolate chips (8 oz.)
1/2 cup nuts

Drop small spoonfuls of dough on greased cookie sheet.
Bake at 350 degrees for 12 minutes.

~~~~~~~~~~~~~~~~~~~~~~~~~~~~~~~~~~~~~~~

"Let's make cookies together, at my house," Mary Beth said to Molly.

"Can we make cookies together?" asked Molly.

"Yes," said Mrs. Peters. "You can work together."

It was time for Scouts to end.
Everyone said the Pee Wee Pledge.

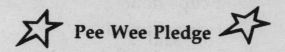

Pee Wee Pledge

We love our country
And our home,
Our school and neighbors too.

As Pee Wee Scouts
We pledge our best
In everything we do.

Then they put their coats on to leave.

"Let's make our cookies now," said Mary Beth on the way home.

"No, they'll be stale by next Tuesday," said Molly. "Let's make them Monday after school."

The next day was Wednesday. During recess Mary Beth walked up to Sonny.

"We're making our cookies together," she told him.

"We are too," said Sonny. "Aren't we, Roger?"

"I s'pose," said Roger.

He was thinking of how warm and soft those cookies were.

He remembered that Mrs. Peters said if boys could eat, boys could cook.

It made sense.

At three o'clock the next Monday the girls hurried to Mary Beth's house.

When they got there, Mary Beth's mother had chocolate chips ready.

She had flour and sugar and eggs out.

"The oven is on," Mrs. Kelly said. "I'll be upstairs. Call me if you need me."

"We will," said Mary Beth.

Molly took the paper out of her pocket. It had the cookie recipe on it.

"Measure the flour," she said.

Mary Beth measured the flour.

She poured it into the bowl.

Molly measured the butter into another bowl.

She put an egg in too.

They both did just what it said on the paper.

First Mary Beth stirred it, and then Molly.

"There is something the matter," said Mary Beth.

Molly looked into the bowl.

"It should be brown," said Mary Beth. "Mrs. Peters's cookies were brown."

"Maybe the chips will make it brown," said Molly.

She dumped the chips in.

It still was not brown.

It was almost white, like flour.

"We need something brown," said Mary Beth, opening the refrigerator.

She reached for a bottle of root beer. It was brown.

"Let's put some of this in," she said.

Molly looked doubtful. It was brown, though.

And the cookie dough did look too white.

She poured some of the root beer into the batter.

Fizzzzz!

Little bubbles were all over.

Molly stirred it.

"It's too runny now," she said. "We need something to make it thick."

Mary Beth looked in the cupboard. She reached for a package of something that had a brown picture on the box.

"What does this say?" she asked.

"Gravy mix," read Molly. "That's good! My mom uses it to make gravy thick when it's too runny. So it would make this thick too."

Mary Beth dumped the box of gravy mix into the cookie dough.

"Perfect!" said Molly. "It's real thick now."

"Thick and brown!" said Mary Beth. "It looks like Mrs. Peters's cookies."

"Now there is more dough," said Molly.

"But not enough chocolate chips!" added Mary Beth.

"I like lots of chocolate chips," said Molly.

"So do I," said Mary Beth. "That's the best part."

The girls looked in the cupboards and in the refrigerator. There were no more chips.

"We need something!" said Mary Beth, stamping her foot.

"These look like chips," said Molly, picking up a plastic bag.

"Dump them in!" said Mary Beth.

The girls stirred and stirred. Then they put the cookies on the pan one at a time, as Mrs. Peters had shown them.

"Terrific!" said Molly. "They look yummy!"

*   *   *

Mary Beth popped the pan into the oven.

She set the timer for twelve minutes.

"Now all we do is wait," she said. "Wait for our yummy yummy cookies."

CHAPTER 4

Baked Frisbees

"**W**ash the dishes when you're through," called Mary Beth's mother from upstairs.

The girls sighed. Cookies were more work than Mrs. Peters had said.

They washed the dishes and then went to Mary Beth's room to wait.

Pretty soon Mary Beth's mother called out, "What is that smell?"

The girls sniffed the air.

"It smells like turkey roasting," said Mrs. Kelly.

"Our cookies!" Molly shouted.

The cookies were not white now.

They were very very brown.

And they were huge.

"They look like hamburgers!" said Molly.

"But they smell like turkey!" said Mary Beth.

Mary Beth's mother came into the kitchen.

She picked up the gravy mix box.

"No wonder it smells like turkey!" she said.

"Why did you use this?"

"The cookies were runny," said Mary Beth.

"From the root beer," said Molly.

"Why did you use root beer?" asked Mary Beth's mother.

"To make them brown," said Molly.

"Baking makes them brown," said Mrs. Kelly.

"It sure does," said Mary Beth.

The girls took the cookies off the pan and put them on a plate.

"They look like giant Frisbees!" cried Mary Beth.

"Or flying saucers," said Molly. "We will never get a badge for these cookies."

"Let's taste one," said Mary Beth.

Mrs. Kelly had gone back upstairs.

Mary Beth took one bite.

She made a terrible face. She ran to the sink and spit it out.

"It's awful!" she said.

"And there is something hard in there."
Mary Beth took a drink of water. "Something real hard," she said.

Molly broke her cookie in half.

She saw little marble-like things inside.

"Yuck!" she said. "I'm not eating these things. They look like beans!"

"Now we won't get our badge," said Mary Beth.

She stamped her foot. She felt mad.

What a waste. They could not even eat the cookies.

"I better go home," said Molly, getting her coat on.

"Take your half of the cookies," said Mary Beth.

"No thanks!" cried Molly. "There's a hex on those cookies, and I didn't put it there!"

CHAPTER 5

Cookie Badges

On Tuesday almost everyone brought a cookie to the meeting.

Some looked like submarines.
Some looked like brown buttons.
Some looked like dog chewies.
But none looked like chocolate chip cookies.

"Today we will try again," said Mrs. Peters.

"Right here. I will not help.

"I will just watch.

"Put in only what it says on the paper."

"That was our mistake," whispered Sonny. "We put in too much other stuff."

"We did too," said Molly.

"I didn't," said Rachel in her running shoes.

"Then why were your cookies so yucky?" asked Roger.

"They weren't yucky," Rachel said. "They just didn't get done. I didn't bake them long enough."

"Dough-face," said Roger. "You're the girl who eats raw dough! Dough-face! Dough-face! Raw-cookie monster Rachel!"

Rachel stuck out her tongue at him.

Each Scout had his or her own bowl. They had their own measuring cups.

They had only the right cookie things.

Mrs. Peters watched them as they made
their cookies.

She put them into the oven.

She set the timer.

This time all the cookies turned out.

Some were big and some were small.

Some were square and some were
round.

Some were oblong.

But they all were soft and warm and had melted chocolate chips in them.

Each Scout gave Mrs. Peters a cookie to taste.

"Wonderful!" she said.

She passed out the cookie badges. The badges were shaped like big cookies. The Scouts pinned them onto their Scout kerchiefs. Then they ate their cookies while Mrs. Peters told them about plans for a skating party.

It was a special party. The Scouts were all supposed to bring their dads.

Everyone looked at Tim Noon.

He didn't have a dad.

Neither did Lisa Ronning or Sonny Betz.

"If you don't have a dad," Mrs. Peters was saying, "you can bring a brother, or an uncle, or even a friend."

"Yikes!" said Rachel. "I get to wear my new figure skates!"

Molly didn't have skates.

Mary Beth had some, but they were black.

Her big brother had outgrown them.

"You can always borrow skates, or rent skates if you don't have any," said Mrs. Peters.

"I have some, Mrs. Peters," called Rachel from across the room. "They are white figure skates. I won't have to borrow or rent any," she said.

"Fine, Rachel," said Mrs. Peters.

Rachel stood on her toes and made skating motions as if she were already on the ice.

"Show-off," muttered Roger. "I'll bet your skates are dumb."

"My skates are what the stars wear to

skate on TV," said Rachel with her hands on her hips.

"A hex on your skates," whispered Molly with her eyes crossed.

"And a hex on chocolate chip cookies," said Mary Beth, moaning. "I ate too many. I don't ever want to see a cookie again in my whole life!"

CHAPTER 6

Dainty Feet

The Pee Wee Scouts counted the days until the skating party. It was on a Saturday afternoon.

It was at the indoor skating rink downtown.

"A hex on school," said Molly Duff on Friday afternoon.

She glared at Mrs. Lane.

First grade was boring sometimes.

Molly knew how to read.

She knew how to spell.

What she didn't know how to do was skate.

They should teach skating in first grade, she thought.

That would be more sensible. Something she didn't know.

Something that was fun.

Chug, chug, chug. The big hand of the clock climbed to the three.

BRRRING! rang the bell at last.

The school day was over.

The skating party was almost here.

In the hall, Molly met Rachel.

She had on her running shoes.

She had on a lavender jacket.

Molly liked lavender. Her mother said it was too fancy a color for first grade.

"It's Ultrasuede," said Rachel when she saw Molly looking at her jacket.

Ultrasuede was very expensive.

No one in first grade had anything Ultrasuede, except Rachel. Rachel's family must have a lot of money, Molly thought.

Rachel turned up the collar on her jacket.

"My dad has figure skates too," said Rachel. "Black ones."

Black-schmack. Rachel's whole family probably were show-offs.

A hex on her father's black figure skates, thought Molly.

She would have to rent skates.

Her father would too.

Even Mary Beth had to rent skates, or wear her brother's black ones.

On Saturday afternoon the Pee Wee

Scouts met at the school. They wore their Pee Wee kerchiefs. Mrs. Peters got rides for the Scouts who needed them.

Rachel was there with her white figure skates.

They had white laces with blue pompoms on them.

The blades were shiny. You could almost see your face in them, like a mirror. They had notches on the end to twirl with.

Her father had black skates. His blades were shiny too.

His black laces had red balls on them.

Just like figure skaters in the Ice Capades on TV.

Lisa Ronning was there with her uncle.

He had a red tassel cap on.

He looked very young. Almost like a brother.

All the fathers and uncles and brothers were laughing together.

In the middle of all of the adults, there was one woman.

"Who is that?" whispered Molly to Mary Beth. "Why is she here?"

People were laughing, and pointing to Sonny.

"It's Sonny's mom!" said Mary Beth. "Sonny brought his *mom* instead of his dad."

"Mrs. Peters said you had to bring a *dad*," said Molly. "Or at least a brother or an uncle!"

Mary Beth nodded. She pulled on her new wool hat.

"Sonny does everything with his mom," she said.

Roger was poking Sonny, and saying,

"Sissy! Bringing your mom to a fathers' skating party!"

Roger was bent over now, laughing.

"My mom can skate," said Sonny. "She can probably skate better than your dad."

"Ha!" said Roger. "We'll see about that."

*   *   *

Roger began to worry about whether his dad could skate.

He wondered if he could skate himself.

He hadn't been skating for over a year.

He was in kindergarten the last time he was on the ice.

Everyone piled into cars.

All the men.

And all the Scouts.

And Mrs. Betz.

When they got to the indoor rink, Mrs. Peters had everyone's tickets ready.

The men went to a counter to rent skates.

The Scouts who did not have their own skates went to another counter, where they could rent children's sizes.

Molly and Mary Beth got in line to rent skates.

Rachel followed them, even though she had skates of her own.

She hung them around her neck by the laces.

The blue pom-poms were bouncing as she walked.

"Your feet are really big," she said to Molly.

"They are not," said Molly quickly.

"What size do you wear?" demanded Rachel.

"I can't remember," lied Molly.

"These are size ten," said Rachel proudly, pointing to her skates. "My mom says ten is a very small size for my age. She says I have dainty feet."

"Size please," said the man behind the counter.

Molly didn't stop to think. "Ten," she said.

"You don't wear ten," said Rachel, pouting.

"I do too," said Molly, taking the skates.

When Mary Beth had rented her skates, the three girls walked over to a bench. They sat down and began to unlace the skates. They put them on.

Mary Beth pulled hers on easily and laced them up.

Rachel pulled hers on carefully and laced them up.

The blades sparkled. The pom-poms danced.

She stood up on the ice in front of Molly and twirled.

*   *   *

Molly's skate wouldn't go on. And it was not white like Rachel's. It was gray. The blades were not like mirrors. They were dull.

She pulled and pulled.

She tugged and tugged.

"Those are too small!" whispered Mary Beth. "Why don't you get a bigger size?"

Molly did not want a bigger size.

She wanted the same size as Rachel.

She did not have big feet.

A hex on Rachel for saying so.

"My socks are too thick," said Molly. "I have to take them off."

She took her socks off and put them into her pocket.

Then she tried to pull the skates on again.

"Your feet are too big," said Rachel.

She stopped twirling and put her hands on her hips.

She stared at Molly's feet.

"They are not!" said Molly, pulling extra hard on the skate.

POP! It went on.

But it felt awful.

Molly's toes were bent. Maybe they were even broken!

Molly could not move one toe. She tried to lace up the skate. She had to pull the lace tightly to tie it.

She pulled and tugged on the other skate to get it on.

Finally it went pop! Her heel slid in. But just barely.

Now all ten toes felt as if they were bent in half.

How would she ever be able to stand up?

Both Rachel and Mary Beth were twirling on the ice.

They reached out their mittened hands to pull her up.

Oof! She was on her feet! The pain from her toes went all the way up her ankles.

"Come on then," said Rachel in her size-ten skates. "Let's skate together."

CHAPTER 7

Crutches

Molly was in the middle.

Rachel had hold of one arm, and Mary Beth had the other.

They skated along, pulling Molly with them.

After a little while Molly could not feel her feet at all.

They were numb!

Molly's dad came skating up to them.

His arms were out.

He wobbled from one side to the other.

His knees bent in, and then out.

"I'm not too good at this," he said, laughing.

Mary Beth's father came skating over to them.

He was better.

But not much better.

He slid toward them.

Crash! He bumped into a bench, and fell onto the ice!

Rachel's father came gliding toward them.

He was skating smoothly. Just like Rachel.

His blades flashed as he came to a stop.

Ice chips flew up where he stood.

Most of the dads were having trouble standing up.

They wobbled back and forth and fell onto the ice.

"Look at Roger and his dad!" cried Rachel. "They are bumping into everyone!"

Mrs. Peters was helping the fathers to their feet.

She was showing them how to put one foot ahead of the other.

She showed some of the Pee Wee Scouts how to stop.

"Look!" called Molly, pointing.

There, skating smoothly among all the wobbling dads, was Mrs. Betz.

In and out, in and out.

Then she skated arm in arm with Sonny.

Then she skated backward.

And then, while everyone watched, Mrs. Betz skated with both arms out and one leg out in back of her. Just like the skaters on TV!

All the dads began to clap. Mrs. Betz bowed and waved.

"See?" said Sonny as he whizzed by Roger. "What did I tell you? I told you my mom could skate better than your dad!"

Roger turned red. He couldn't call Sonny a sissy now.

He and his mother could outskate them all!

"Hex, hex, hex," called Molly to Sonny and his mom.

Her feet were aching. She felt awful.

"Try this!" said Rachel, skating with one leg out in front of her.

Molly tried it and toppled over sideways.

"Come on, Molly!" they called. "You're no fun today!"

Molly got to her feet.

She closed her eyes in pain, and tried again to put one leg out in front of her. It did not work.

She turned her ankle and fell on the ice.

"I can't walk!" she said, trying to get to her feet.

When her father pulled her up, she could not stand on her sore ankle.

"It's broken!" she cried.

Everyone ran to help.

They carried Molly to the bench.

Mrs. Peters showed them how to make a stretcher with a coat, and they took her to the car.

Molly's father began to take her skates off.

Molly cried in pain.

"Let's wait," said Mrs. Peters, who always took charge. "It is best not to disturb a patient."

Molly could not believe what was happening to her.

Her father's car was taking her to the hospital!

Was her ankle really broken?

She should not have lied about her skate size.

A hex on size ten!

At the hospital everyone got out.

They followed the coat-stretcher.

It looked like a parade.

In the emergency room a nurse X-rayed Molly's ankle.

The doctor came in and felt Molly's bones.

He looked at the X rays.

"It is not broken," he said. "Just sprained. You have a sprained ankle, Molly. You will have to stay off it for a while."

The doctor wrapped her ankle with a bandage.

Then he got out a pair of crutches and showed Molly how to walk on them.

In the waiting room all the Scouts gathered around Molly.

"Wow!" said Roger. "Real crutches!"

"My brother had crutches once," said Mary Beth.

Rachel was standing in back by the door.

No one was fussing over her shiny skates now.

No one was noticing her blue pom-poms.

Rachel had never sprained her ankle.

She had never had crutches.

"Does it hurt?" asked Sonny.

"Put ice on it," said his mother.

"We must get Molly home and into a warm bed," said Mrs. Peters.

Everyone followed Molly out.
She led the parade, on her crutches.

CHAPTER 8

A Badge for Molly

Molly went to bed.

She had to miss school.

Everyone sent her cards.

The Pee Wee Scouts made their own cards.

Roger's had a girl skating on it.

It did not look like Molly. But Molly liked it.

Mary Beth drew a hospital bed on hers.

And she brought Molly candy. Chocolate-covered cherries!

Her favorites.

Mrs. Peters sent flowers, from the whole Pee Wee Scout Troop.

They made Molly's room look bright and cheery.

Every day after school some of the Scouts came to her house.

They played Candy Land.

Mary Beth brought Molly her homework and her school papers.

They wrote spelling words together.

"I wish I had a sprained ankle," said Rachel when she came to visit.

"You skate too well," said Molly. "You wouldn't fall on the ice."

"I used to fall when I was little," admitted Rachel. "It took me a long time to learn."

Molly wished she hadn't hexed Rachel.

And the good skaters.

It took time to learn to skate.

She could learn to skate too.

Once she got the right size skates.

The next week Molly went back to school.

She went on her crutches.

On Tuesday she went to Pee Wee Scouts on her crutches.

"I have some badges to give out," said Mrs. Peters. "Some of you get a skating badge."

Everyone clapped when the good skaters got their badges.

They all pinned them on their Scout kerchiefs or their shirts.

Next to their cookie badges.

The skating badge showed a picture of a skate.

A skate with no pom-poms.

Just a plain skate.

"I'll get that badge someday," said Molly.

"Of course," said Mrs. Peters.

"And now I have another badge. It is a badge for being a good patient."

Everyone knew who that badge was for!

The Pee Wee Scouts all looked at Molly.

"Molly Duff," said Mrs. Peters. "Come up and get your badge please."

Molly got up.

She walked to the front of the room on her crutches.

"Thank you," she said as she pinned it onto her blouse.

The badge was beautiful.
It had a little bed on it.
It looked like Molly's bed!

Across the bed was a little thermometer.

Around the edge it said THE GOOD PATIENT BADGE.

Molly hobbled back to her chair.

Everyone clapped.

She was glad to have a badge to pin on next to her cookie badge.

It wasn't as good as a skating badge.

But almost!